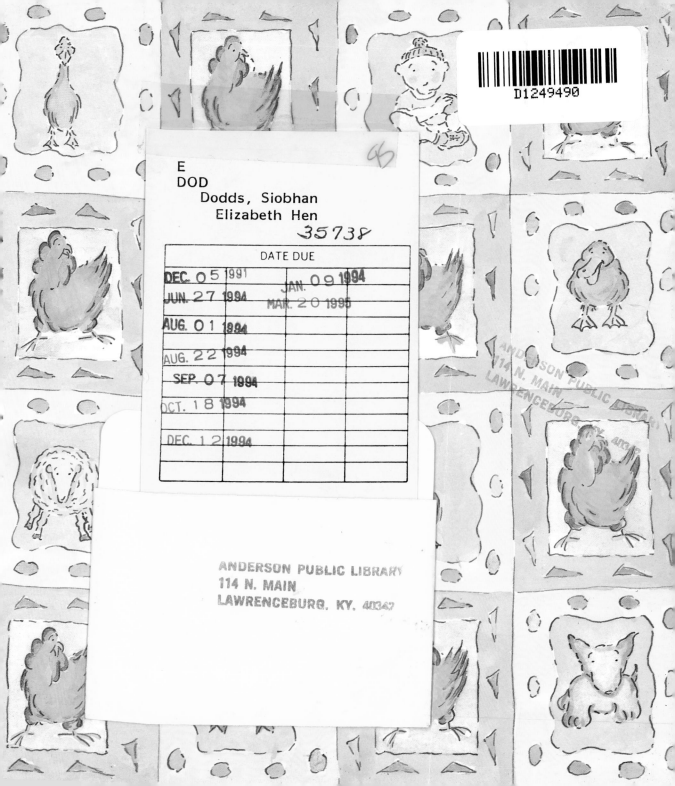

Elizabeth Hen

Siobhan Dodds

Joy Street Books
Little, Brown and Company
Boston / Toronto

For Fiona

First U.S. Edition

Library of Congress Cataloging-in-Publication Data
Dodds, Siobhan.
  Elizabeth Hen.

  Summary: The reader may count the animals as Elizabeth
shares her news with them that she has laid an egg.
  [1. Domestic animals—Fiction.   2. Counting]
I. Title.
PZ7.D6629El   1987   [E]   87-14344
ISBN 0-316-18818-2

Copyright © 1987 by Siobhan Dodds
First published in Great Britain in 1987 by
Orchard Books
Printed and bound in Italy

One day Elizabeth Hen laid an egg.

Feeling very proud,
she went to tell her friends.
First she told the cow
with her two calves,

then the sheep
with her three lambs,

and then the goose
with her four goslings.

Next she told the farmer's wife
with her five children,

the cat with her six kittens,

the pig with her seven piglets,

then the dog
with her eight puppies,

and the duck
with her nine ducklings.

Last of all she told the rabbit
with her ten babies.

But when Elizabeth Hen
returned to her egg,
something strange was happening.

The egg was cracked
and rocking from side to side.
TAP-TAP-TAP! went the egg.
Out popped a chick!

Elizabeth Hen was as proud as could be.

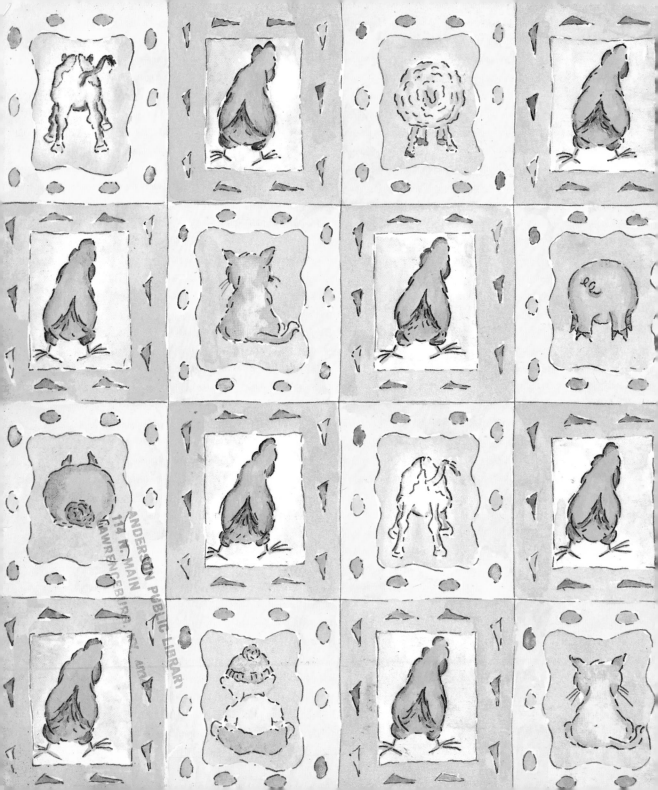